W9-AYD-682

Disney's

American Frontier #6

DAVY CROCKETT
AND THE HIGHWAYMEN
A Historical Novel

By Ron Fontes and Justine Korman
Illustrations by Charlie Shaw
Cover illustration by Dave Henderson

DISNEP PRESS

NEW YORK

Look for these other books in the
American Frontier series:

Calamity Jane at Fort Sanders

Davy Crockett and the Creek Indians

Davy Crockett and the King of the River

Davy Crockett and the Pirates at Cave-in Rock

Davy Crockett at the Alamo

Johnny Appleseed and the Planting of the West

Sacajawea and the Journey to the Pacific

FIRST EDITION
1   3   5   7   9   10   8   6   4   2

Library of Congress Catalog Card Number: 92-52975
ISBN: 1-56282-260-8/1-56282-261-6 (lib. bdg.)

Consultant: Judith A. Brundin, Supervisory Education Specialist
National Museum of the American Indian
Smithsonian Institution, New York

CHAPTER 1

Davy Crockett smelled the wood burning in his neighbor's stove and saw the smoke rise like a lazy snake over the green trees in the next hollow. He frowned. Bean's Creek was becoming too crowded, and it was time for him to find a new place for his family to settle. Davy could never stay in any one place for very long. The itch to explore fresh, open land would begin to overtake him, and as soon as he started smelling the smoke from his neighbor's stove, he knew it was time to move on.

It wasn't that Davy was not a neighborly man. If someone needed to put up a barn, Davy was there to help. If a fence needed mending, Davy would pitch right in. If a neighbor was a little scarce of meat during the winter, Davy would hunt up a deer. In fact, Davy would give folks the shirt off his back, and he often did.

Davy watched the smoke for one more minute, then swung his ax above his head and brought it down with a sharp *crack!* on a thick hickory log. The log split in two.

Across the cornfield, Davy saw his wife, Polly, carrying a leather bucket of water. He smiled at her as she started toward him.

Davy thought Polly was still as pretty as the day they'd met. She had smooth dark hair coiled in neat braids under her faded sunbonnet, and her pink calico dress was the same color as the flowers blooming on the path up to their cabin. The Crocketts' baby daughter, Margaret, bounced on Polly's hip.

Davy's sons, Billy and Johnny, sang an old folk song as they worked in the field, weeding rows of tender young corn. Davy's prize hunting dogs, Whirlwind, Bullet, and Blue, dozed on the porch of the Crocketts' log cabin.

Davy put down his ax and wiped the sweat from his brow as Polly handed him a tin cup filled with cool water. He gulped the water, then handed the cup back for a refill.

"Don't exert yourself too much, Davy," Polly warned. "You're still getting over that swamp fever."

"I feel as frisky as a fox in a chicken coop!" Davy declared.

Polly smiled, but there was a hint of worry in her blue eyes. A few weeks earlier, while Davy was away on a hunting trip, a neighbor had come to the cabin to tell her that Davy had taken sick in the woods.

Polly could not control her joy at the sight of her husband coming up the path to the cabin the next day. Even though he was dazed with swamp fever, Davy called the neighbor's story a whopper of a lie. But he then spent all the next week in bed, and Polly was still fretting over him. "That's enough wood for now," she told her husband. "Maybe you should rest."

But Davy shook his head. "Can't go leaving you and the young'uns without enough wood for the stove."

"I don't think you should scout for a new homestead so soon after your fever," Polly said.

"Now, now," Davy soothed. "You know as well as I do we've got to be moving on. And the spring is the best time to go scouting for a new place.

"I know this is fine country right here," Davy told Polly. "But with all the marshes around, sooner or later you and the young'uns might come down with swamp fever, too."

Polly sighed. "I just hate to think of you being gone again."

Davy put his arm around Polly's shoulders and tickled Margaret's smooth cheek. "I won't be gone long," he promised. "The heavy planting's done. All you and the boys will have to do is keep the garden weeded and pick enough for your supper. I'll be home in time for the big harvest. And by then I'll have a new cabin built and ready for the winter."

Polly wasn't keen on moving again, but she knew there was no talking Davy out of an idea once he'd made up his mind.

"Once I find us the right place, we'll settle for good," Davy assured her. And Polly smiled at last.

"Will there be a school for the boys and Margaret?" Polly asked.

"There'll be a school," Davy said. "And plenty of game to

hunt," he added with a gleam in his eyes. Davy loved hunting, but lately so many folks had been settling near Bean's Creek that hardly any game was left nearby. With each hunting trip, Davy had to go farther from home just to fill his game bag.

"Where will we go this time?" Polly wondered, shifting the baby on her hip.

"Well, there isn't room to swing a cat back east. Reckon we'll go west. Folks say that the new territory is a paradise," Davy replied. A new treaty with the Chickasaw tribe had granted more land to settlers in western Tennessee.

Polly knew the dreamy look in Davy's eyes. New frontiers were calling to him, and he always answered the call.

"How soon will you leave?" Polly asked.

"Soon as I fill the woodbox and pack my saddlebags," Davy said. But Polly persuaded him to spend a few more days with her and the children until she was sure he was over his fever.

CHAPTER 2

The weather was still sunny on the morning Georgie Russel came galloping up to the Crockett cabin on his white horse, Soapy. Georgie had been Davy's good friend for as long as anyone could remember. His merry blue eyes peeked out from beneath a flat brown hat, and well-worn buckskins hung loosely over his tall, rangy frame. Georgie balanced a Kentucky hunting rifle in the crook of his arm.

Davy's black horse, Lightning, stamped restlessly beside Soapy as Davy said good-bye to his family. Then he eased up into his saddle and settled his own rifle, Old Betsy, across his arm. He called a last farewell to Polly. "Keep the hearth warm!"

Polly chuckled. "You left me enough wood to last till Christmas—but you better not stay gone that long, Mr. Crockett!"

"Don't kill all the bears till we get there!" Johnny shouted.

"And steer clear of any highwaymen. Those thieves can be dangerous," Polly added.

"Keep your sights clean, fellers," Georgie told the young

Crocketts. "We'll be back soon!" he promised Polly.

"With more of your outrageous stories about Davy?" Polly teased.

"You betcha," Georgie said. Then he spurred Soapy down the path behind Davy.

"Take care of your ma," Davy called to Billy and Johnny.

The boys waved and waved until long after their father's horse had vanished into the thick woods.

Davy and Georgie rode west. The sun warmed their backs all morning, then shone in their eyes during the long afternoon as they ambled across Tennessee.

The woodsmen heard mockingbirds and mourning doves call and coo in the trees around them. The birds fell silent at the approach of the horses, then resumed their cries and chatter once Lightning and Soapy had passed.

Davy looked up at hickory branches decorated with feathery flowers that would turn to tasty nuts in the fall. Fat gray squirrels scampered from branch to branch. Davy knew that a place so thick with small game was likely to have its share of bobcats, bears, and deer, too.

Georgie teased a mockingbird with the call of a Tennessee thrush, then with the cry of a blue jay. The mockingbird answered each call in kind. Davy added his own voice until the whole woods resounded with chattering birds.

"Well, how about this place, Davy?" Georgie asked.

Davy stroked his chin thoughtfully. "Mighty pretty country," he agreed. "But we're still too close to Bean's Creek. A

man has to have room to stretch. 'Sides, the Chickasaw still live in these parts. We've been followed for the last couple of miles."

Georgie looked around nervously.

"Don't worry," Davy said. "They enjoyed your birdcalls as much as you enjoyed theirs."

Georgie blushed. "Why didn't you..."

"Now, Georgie, settle down. The Chickasaw won't bother us if we don't bother them," Davy said.

Georgie pushed his hat back and scratched his head. "Reckon I could use a few more days riding, anyhow. I'm not near sore enough to quit yet!"

So on they rode until four days later, when they came to the gurgling headwaters of a creek in a lush wood thick with trees and full of game. Deer scattered at the sound of the approaching horses.

A flock of wild turkeys gobbled through the underbrush, and a cardinal swooped by in a streak of brilliant red. Chipmunks chattered at the roots of trees, and crawfish did their funny backward swim in the rushing creek.

Davy saw two fat bears wrestling in the clear water. They lumbered onto the banks and shook their thick fur.

"You going any farther?" Davy asked his friend.

Georgie grinned. "Not me. I like it fine right here!"

"Well, now, I calculate we're not far from the Natchez Trace," Davy said. The famous trail was originally blazed by local tribes but was later used by tradesmen. The traders sailed south with their goods on the Mississippi River, and, once

they had sold everything—including their boats—they returned north by foot or on horseback on the Trace.

Georgie squirmed in his saddle and rubbed his flank. "Wouldn't that be a mite crowded for you, Davy? Lots of travelers pass this way."

"True enough," Davy said. "But travelers are traveling, not staying put. Maybe I could open an inn, like my daddy. I always did enjoy hearing and telling stories with the folks passing through."

Davy and Georgie set up camp on a rise with a view of the creek and the distant hills. Then they wasted no time clearing the land. Davy peeled off his buckskin shirt, spit on his hands, and started whacking the trunk of a sweet gum tree with his heavy ax. Wood chips smacked against his leggings and stuck to his chest and arms.

The rich hills of Tennessee were crowded not only with sweet gum trees but with cottonwoods, pecan trees, and several kinds of oak. Davy decided to leave a tall pecan tree standing. He knew Polly made the best pecan pie.

Georgie chopped the branches off each fallen sweet gum and hitched the logs to Soapy and Lightning. The horses dragged each heavy log to the spot Davy had marked for his cabin, then Georgie unhitched the horses and began to cut notches in the logs.

But Georgie stopped after the first swing of the heavy, hoelike tool. He had suddenly remembered that there were new rules for homesteading. Folks now had to register their property. He sure hoped no one else had already claimed this land. He and Davy might have done all this work for nothing.

Georgie rubbed his callused hands as he nervously asked, "Hey, Davy, ain't we forgot something?"

Davy straightened up and wiped the sweat from his brow. "I reckon not. We're facing west, like Polly wanted."

"I don't mean this cabin," Georgie said. "We ain't filed our claims on this land yet."

Davy was shocked. "You mean you can't just take the parcel you want?"

"Not since they opened this new territory. It's got to be filed legally," Georgie explained. He wished he'd remembered that sooner.

Davy scratched his head. "Well, where do we go to do that?"

Georgie shrugged. "Nearest settlement, I reckon."

Davy picked up his shirt. "This country's getting almighty civilized," he said, and he scrambled to a high branch of the pecan tree. The greenish yellow flowers hung like a fringe from the twigs and sprinkled seeds on Davy's buckskins as he pulled himself up for a view.

Davy's keen brown eyes scanned the rolling hills. To the north, he could just make out the smoke rising from several chimneys. "Reckon the village is a couple of miles north," he called down to Georgie.

"Reckon I was just getting over my saddle sores," Georgie grumbled. He patted Soapy's nose and held the horse steady as he swung the leather saddle onto its back.

Davy and Georgie started out for the settlement. By the time Georgie had finished singing about Davy's exploits—wrestling a bobcat, grinning down a raccoon, and hugging a she-bear—the two men had reached the small village nestled between the hills. A log wall enclosed a general store, a church, a blacksmith's forge, a one-room school, and a few houses.

"Polly will like this place," Davy said. "She's been wanting to send Johnny and Billy to school."

Davy and Georgie rode to the general store, which was the biggest building in the settlement. It had real glass in the windows, and sacks and barrels crowded the porch.

A man came out of the building and hastily closed the door. He had a weathered, kindly face and wore an old-fashioned three-cornered hat and a gray leather vest over a white shirt and knee britches. The man nodded quickly at Davy and Georgie, then hurried past.

"Hold on there, mister!" Davy called.

The man stopped impatiently.

"Who do we see about filing a claim on some land?" Davy asked.

"Me, Elmo Swaney, but you'll have to wait. I'm judging the shooting match today," the man snapped.

Davy grinned at Georgie. "Shooting match? Any objection to a couple of strangers buying in?"

Mr. Swaney looked the two woodsmen up and down.

"Save your money. You'll be shooting against Wildman Farley."

Georgie struggled not to laugh. Davy had never lost a shooting match.

Shots boomed in the distance. Mr. Swaney scowled and looked toward the sound.

"Sounds like they started without you," Georgie said.

Mr. Swaney rushed away, with Davy and Georgie at his heels.

CHAPTER 3

The echo of gunshot still rang in the air as Davy and Georgie reached a fenced-in field. Sixty yards across the flat land, white paper targets were tacked to boards nailed to posts.

A farmer in a dusty homespun shirt and trousers stepped back from the log that marked the firing line. His face was set in a deep frown as he cradled his smoking rifle in his arms.

Two other men behind the log looked just as unhappy as they leaned on their long rifles and watched a rough-looking bull of a man plant his huge feet behind the firing line. The big man raised a rifle inlaid with fancy silver scrollwork.

The man was Wildman Farley. He had black bushy hair and beady eyes, and his lined face was framed by scruffy black sideburns. His arms were almost as huge as his legs, which were as thick as tree trunks.

The small audience of spectators shrank from Farley's gaze. Only the lone cow hitched to a fence post seemed indifferent to his angry black eyes.

Across the field, Farley's cronies, Bruno and Henderson, lounged at a safe distance from the target posts. Tall, bony Bruno stooped like a vulture. A sparse brown beard studded his sunken cheeks like straw on a badly stuffed scarecrow. Shorter and stockier, but equally nasty looking, was Henderson.

Farley grunted at the arrival of Swaney, Davy, and Georgie. The newcomers had distracted him from his shot. He looked crossly over his shoulder.

Mr. Swaney scolded, "You should've waited for me, Wildman."

The large man scowled. "You weren't here," he rumbled. He looked Davy and Georgie up and down, then, deciding they were beneath his notice, he turned back to the target and fired.

The sharp smell of gunpowder hung in the air while smoke from the gun's firing pan curled around Farley's face.

With the blast still echoing across the field, Bruno and Henderson hurried to the target post. The target was a six-inch square with a **V** cut in the exact center of the paper. The paper on the other target was pierced slightly above and just under the points of the **V**. The bullet on Farley's target had struck to the left of the point.

But Bruno called, in his reedy, nasal voice, "Right in the notch, Wildman!"

Henderson tore the paper off Farley's target and tossed it into the woods.

Farley turned to the three other marksmen in triumph. "That's the last round. The cow stays mine, and you'd all best turn over your cash."

Mr. Swaney objected. "Now wait a minute! This ain't fair judging!" He pointed to the targets. "Those men are friends of yours."

Bruno pointed to the other marksmen. "Don't hear no complaints, do you?"

Mr. Swaney and Davy looked at the three men digging through their pockets for money. They were obviously angry but afraid to say anything.

Mr. Swaney's glance fell on the black brand burned onto the cow's flank. "Hold on there, Wildman. You can't use someone else's property to stake your bet."

"Who says the cow ain't mine?" Farley rumbled. "Can't a man buy a cow around here?"

Bruno and Henderson chuckled until Farley shot them an angry glance.

Mr. Swaney shrugged his shoulders, seeming to shrink under the hostile challenge in Farley's eyes.

The big man turned his back on Mr. Swaney and started toward the three men to collect his winnings.

"How much do you figure that cow is worth?" Davy called after him.

Farley turned a contemptuous gaze on Davy and said, "Fifteen dollars, cash money. Why?"

Davy pulled out a jingling leather pouch. "Never went to

a shooting match in my life without at least gettin' one shot off," he drawled. "I'll bet cash against yer cow, same as those fellers."

Farley agreed, "One shot it is. If I win, you pay me fifteen dollars."

Davy nodded. "And if I do, I get the cow, and we all keep our own money."

Farley laughed. "Hey, Bruno," he called, "charge up my rifle."

Bruno nodded, his giant Adam's apple bobbing in his scrawny neck. Henderson sneered at Davy, who looked right back at him and smiled.

Davy emptied the pouch into his palm and counted out nine gold coins. Georgie gave him the other six.

Davy handed the money to Mr. Swaney and said, "Take care of these here cartwheels. And this time *you* do the judgin'."

CHAPTER 4

Davy placed the butt of his Kentucky hunting rifle on the ground, then poured gunpowder from his powder horn down the barrel. He wrapped a round lead ball in a patch of deerskin and pushed it down the barrel with the tamping rod. Now he was ready for the shoot.

Mr. Swaney walked to the target tree, followed by Henderson.

Bruno handed Farley his fancy Pennsylvania rifle. Sunlight glinted on the silver scrollwork decorating the shiny barrel.

Davy looked at the weapon. Pennsylvania rifles were the finest, made by immigrant German gunsmiths who took great pride in their work. "That's a mighty fancy shootin' iron for this part of the woods," he said.

Farley's grin exposed his big yellow teeth. "Yeah—ain't it?" he said in a taunting voice.

Farley planted his huge feet on the firing line and looked toward the target, where Mr. Swaney had put two new pieces of paper on the board. He raised his rifle, took careful aim, and fired.

Henderson and Mr. Swaney looked at Farley's target. The bullet had struck the top of the **V**. Henderson grinned.

Mr. Swaney reported with a note of disappointment, "Dead center for Wildman!"

The huge man stepped back from the firing line, triumphant. Davy, calm as a summer day, aimed briefly and fired.

Mr. Swaney and Henderson once more moved in to examine the target. Henderson's wide face fell. Mr. Swaney turned and called out happily, "This one's dead center, too. You'll have to fire another round."

Farley was surprised and not at all pleased. "Ah, you was lucky," he grumbled.

Davy didn't say anything, but only reloaded his rifle. When Davy glanced Georgie's way, he saw his friend struggling to not burst out laughing.

Farley stepped angrily up to the log, carefully aimed, and fired again.

Henderson examined the target and smiled. Farley's bullet was less than an inch left of his first shot.

Mr. Swaney shouted, "Less'n a finger off the notch!"

Farley stepped back from the firing line and said to Davy, "Better save your powder, stranger."

Davy ignored Farley. He licked his thumb and rubbed his sight clean. Then he sighted and fired with swift precision.

Mr. Swaney and Henderson checked the target but saw no sign of Davy's second shot—only the dead center hole of his first.

Mr. Swaney looked confused. Henderson laughed. He folded his thick arms across his chest with satisfaction.

"Didn't even cut paper!" Farley taunted.

"I was afraid you fired too fast," Georgie told his friend gently.

"Let's take a look," Davy suggested. And they walked across the field.

Puzzled by not finding Davy's second bullet, Mr. Swaney leaned close to the board. He examined the single hole in the target and probed it with his pocketknife.

Farley came puffing up to the post along with Davy, Georgie, and the three other marksmen.

Farley's laugh boomed. "He missed the whole blamed board!"

Mr. Swaney dug deeper into the wooden target. "I ain't so sure."

Mr. Swaney's knife blade pried a bullet from the hole— and then a second bullet from deeper inside! Mr. Swaney held up both bullets. "Lookee here—one bullet right on top of the other."

Georgie slapped his thigh. "Yahoo! That's the kinda shootin' makes the ol' raccoon squeal!"

Farley glowered. He untied the cow and stomped over to Davy. His fists clenched with fury, he handed over the tether.

"Thank you kindly," Davy replied with a grin.

One of the defeated marksmen let out a joyous whoop. But his cry died in midyell at one glance from Farley. The other marksmen did their best to stifle their smiles. But not any of the spectators, even Mr. Swaney, could help chuckling to themselves.

CHAPTER 5

Davy and Georgie left the shooting field with Mr. Swaney. All the way back to his store, the older man expressed his amazement at Davy's victory.

"I don't know if you were lucky or you're the best shot since Davy Crockett, but I'm sure glad you happened by today," Mr. Swaney gushed.

Georgie winked at Davy, who might have introduced himself if the man hadn't quickly rattled on. "Did my heart good to see Wildman lose for a change," Mr. Swaney said.

The three men reached the general store, where Davy and Georgie had first seen Mr. Swaney. He pointed to a rough log hitching post. "You can hitch your cow and your horses here," he said. "I only hope the cow was really Wildman's to lose." He shook his head. "I'll go dig out the survey map so we can see about your land," he said as he went into the store.

Davy looked up from tying the cow's tether around the hitching post and noticed a farmer coming toward him from across the town square. The farmer seemed angry.

"That's my cow!" he shouted. "See? That's my brand."

Davy looked at the black mark burned on the cow's flank. He shrugged and explained, "I can't say as I'm well acquainted with this particular critter. I just won her from Wildman Farley in a shooting contest."

The farmer trembled when he heard Wildman's name. He backed away from Davy as if he might get burned.

Davy held up his hand and said, "Hold on, friend. I've just come here, and I ain't even got a cabin, much less a barn. Why don't you take this cow on home?" He turned the tether over to the grateful farmer, who led his cow home.

Davy and Georgie turned and went inside Mr. Swaney's general store, which also served as the town hall and the post office. Rows of seven shelves held bags of flour and jugs of molasses, books, hats, hammers and nails, powder and shot, paper and slates. Penny candy jars and a pickle barrel rested in front of the counter. Several racks of antlers adorned the rough log walls.

Mr. Swaney nodded and pointed to a spot near the curving blue line of the creek. "Sounds like here's where your claim is on the survey map. You're the first one in, over them parts. Your nearest neighbor is a Cherokee named Charley Two Shirts. He's a nice feller with a family."

Davy and Georgie nodded with satisfaction.

"Now just sign these," Mr. Swaney said, sliding papers across the rough table. He dipped a quill pen in a bottle of ink.

Mr. Swaney glanced at the signature on the form. "*Davy Crockett!* Are you *the* Davy Crockett?"

Davy nodded modestly. "Why, yes, I am."

Mr. Swaney marveled, "No wonder you beat Wildman!"

Georgie grinned. "He wasn't too happy about it, was he?"

Mr. Swaney agreed. "Wildman ain't used to things goin' against him. He's got folks pretty well buffaloed around here," he said as he carefully signed the claim and put it away.

"So I noticed," Davy remarked. He was thinking of the farmer and his cow.

Mr. Swaney sighed. "We had the beginning of a purty decent little community here before Wildman and his riffraff moved in on us."

"Bears don't come snuffin' around a tree unless there's honey in it," Davy said. "What are they doing around here?"

Mr. Swaney glanced around the empty store nervously and lowered his voice. "Nobody dares talk about it, but Wildman's gang has been running the Indians off their land and selling it to newcomers who don't know any better."

Davy bristled. "They can't do that! The government guaranteed that land to the Indians by treaty."

Mr. Swaney laughed bitterly. "Treaties don't mean nothin' to Wildman."

"Why doesn't somebody stop him?" asked Georgie.

"Feller that was magistrate here tried. He went over to see Wildman and his gang and never came back!" Mr. Swaney said. "Magistrate had the purtiest rifle ever seen in these parts. Nobody knows what happened to him, but we know where his gun is."

Georgie nodded grimly. "Wildman was shooting with it today."

Mr. Swaney said, "That's right." He turned to Davy. "Crockett, you're the only man I'd ask to stand up to Wildman's gang. Will you take the job of magistrate?"

Davy asked, "What-all would I have to do?"

"Get us some law and order around here," Mr. Swaney said. "Write out warrants and bring that bunch in for trial!"

Davy rubbed his chin thoughtfully. "I've never read a page of the law in my life."

Mr. Swaney smiled. "All the better. We don't need fancy words, just an honest man with common sense."

Davy said uncertainly, "Well, I ain't crawfishin', but I kinda got my hands full. I got to finish my cabin so I can bring my family out before winter."

"This is no fit place fer families while these varmints are running loose. What do you say?" Mr. Swaney pleaded.

Davy still hadn't decided. He had to be sure he was right before he could go ahead.

CHAPTER 6

Soon Davy and Georgie were again hard at work on the claim, squaring timbers with their heavy broad axes.

Georgie stopped to wipe the sweat from his forehead. He picked up a drinking gourd, but the hollowed-out squash shell was empty.

"I'm drier'n a powder horn," Georgie complained.

Davy nodded. "Yeah, would you fetch me some water, too?" he asked. Then he lifted his ax again.

Georgie walked down the hill toward a small stream. He could practically taste the cold, clear water rushing in the stony bed beyond the canebrake on its banks. Georgie thrashed through on the reed, then stopped. Something was stirring in the brush.

Georgie peered through leaves and stalks and caught a glimpse of straight black hair and buckskins. Then the figure vanished into the canebrake.

Georgie glanced nervously back in Davy's direction. He figured he ought to warn Davy. Holding his hands up to his mouth, he signaled Davy by whistling the call of the Tennessee thrush.

Davy heard the signal and knew what it meant—trouble! He picked up the two rifles leaning against a nearby tree and headed silently toward the stream.

Georgie watched the canebrake intently as he waited for his friend. Davy approached as quiet as snow and handed Georgie his rifle.

Georgie pointed to a spot in the thick reeds, and the two woodsmen advanced cautiously.

Davy prodded the dense stalks with the long barrel of his gun. The rifle parted the stems to reveal two terrified Cherokee children huddling against their frightened mother. The mother's strong arms circled tightly around her children.

Davy was surprised. He thought suddenly of Polly, the boys, and little Margaret. He smiled gently at the frightened woman. Then Davy looked back at Georgie and asked, "This what stood your hair up?"

Before Georgie could answer, a young Cherokee warrior leapt out of the canebrake. His face showed his determination to defend his family, but he was unarmed and had obviously suffered a beating.

Davy put down his gun and held up his hands. "We're not going to hurt you or your kin," he said gently.

The warrior studied Davy's face, then glanced briefly at Georgie's rifle. Georgie dropped the gun like a hot potato.

"See? Friends!" Georgie said hastily to the warrior.

The Cherokee looked deep into Georgie's blue eyes, then gave a small, cautious nod. He was a short but solidly built man. His cotton shirt was torn, and his round face and arms were bruised. Blood trickled from a cut across his cheekbone.

"Who are you?" Davy asked.

"I am Charley Two Shirts," the man replied.

"Why, he's your neighbor!" Georgie exclaimed, surprise mixing with relief.

"What happened to you?" Davy asked.

"Three white men came to my farm," Charley Two Shirts explained. "They told me to clear out. But I said, 'This is my land.' And they said, 'Indians have no land.'"

"Then we fought," Charley continued. "But there were three of them, and one was as big as a bear."

Davy's fists clenched and his jaw tightened. He looked at Charley's wife and children, who had emerged quietly from the brush. The children were still frightened, but their mother seemed to understand that Davy and Georgie were friendly. And Davy aimed to prove it. Now his mind was made up.

"That tears it!" Davy declared. "If a man can't live a peaceable life on his own land, reckon I'll take that magistrate job right now!"

Georgie nodded. "I'm with you, Davy. I'd be right pleased to help you write out those warrants!"

"Save the writing for later. We'll deliver these warrants

verbally!" Davy said. He turned to Charley's wife and said, "Missus Two Shirts, you and the young'uns go on to our camp and make yourselves at home." To Charley he said, "Come on! Let's go back to that farm of yours!"

CHAPTER 7

Davy, Georgie, and Charley Two Shirts walked across a cornfield to Charley's clay-plastered log cabin. Smoke curled from the chimney. Three horses were tethered out front.

"Let's pay a call on your uninvited company, Charley," said Davy.

Bruno was lazing on the porch, sipping from a jug. His feet dropped off the railing when he saw Davy and Georgie's rifles. He leaned into the cabin door and screeched a warning to Farley.

Farley shoved Bruno aside as he strode onto the cabin's porch brandishing his fancy rifle. Bruno and Henderson scrambled to follow him, rifles in hand.

Georgie already had his finger on the trigger, but Davy balanced his rifle casually across his arm.

Davy saw the deep anger in Farley's black eyes. The huge man was still smoldering because Davy had beat him in the shooting match.

"Looking for somebody?" Farley shouted.

Davy spoke calmly. "Yeah," he said. "The men that run my friend here off his land."

Farley growled. "Since when is Davy Crockett a friend of Injuns?"

Davy and Georgie exchanged glances.

"That's right," Farley said. "I know who you are. Nothing gets by me. So tell me, Davy Crockett, since when are you a friend of Injuns?"

Davy explained patiently, "I've always been a friend of the Cherokee people. I've got no bone to pick with any Indian tribe since we signed a peace with 'em."

Farley stepped to the railing. "Get this straight, Crockett. These yarns they tell about you don't scare me none. This land's too good for Injuns. I'm filing a claim on it!"

Davy answered quietly but sternly, "No, you ain't! This man's got rights, just the same as everybody."

"Take a powerful lot of argument to convince me of that," said Farley.

"That's what I come for," Davy answered.

Farley's harsh laugh seemed to echo off the hills. "Why, I've eaten better men than you whole, with their heads buttered and their ears pinned back!" He handed his fancy rifle to Bruno.

"Now, I'm fresh out of butter, but I'm sure we can solve this like reasonable men," Davy began, but before he could say more, Farley leapt off the porch and landed right in front of him. Farley swung a meaty fist; Davy ducked.

He came up grinning. "I'd rather talk this out," he said, "but if it's a fight you want, Wildman, let's set the rules."

"Rough and tumble, no holds barred!" Farley shouted, eagerly jabbing the air.

Davy tossed his rifle to Charley, took off his powder horn, and unbuckled his belt. He usually left the bragging to Georgie, but starting a fight without a brag would be as rude as digging into your supper without saying grace. So he let fly.

"It's only fair to warn you, Wildman," he boasted, "I'm half horse and half alligator, with a touch of snappin' turtle. I can hug a bear too close for comfort and shoot the tail off a kite in a March wind!"

Farley screwed up his face and bellowed, "I'm the original iron-jawed, brass-mounted, copper-bellied corpse maker. Stand back and give me room! I'm gonna turn myself loose!"

Wildman spit on his dusty hands and rubbed them together. Bruno and Henderson whooped with glee.

Davy held his fists high and balanced lightly on the balls of his feet. He had wrestled tougher bears than Farley. Bullies like him usually just needed a good sting on the nose to make them back down.

Farley swung, and Davy ducked and delivered a punch of his own. His fist rocked Farley's jaw. Farley spit red and rushed at Davy like an angry bull. Davy met his charge with another punch. Farley shook it off and began swinging his arms like the paddle wheels of a steamboat.

Davy fought back, peppering Farley with punches, but they only served to rile the huge man more.

Georgie pounded his fist against his palm as he watched the battle. He knew Davy was a great fighter, but his friend sure looked like he could use some help.

Charley hoped Davy wouldn't be too badly hurt. His own face still stung from Farley's beating.

Davy and Farley fought up, down, sideways, and all around the farmyard while the chickens squawked and the dust flew. Their grunts and groans and punches boomed in the quiet.

Farley hauled back with his giant boot and kicked Davy square in the stomach. Davy doubled over.

Bruno shouted, "Now you got him!"

Farley grabbed Davy and flipped him onto his shoulders like a sack of flour. Then he started spinning like a tornado.

Helpless as a rabbit in a trap, Davy watched the world twirl. Then Farley let him go, and Davy flew through the air and crashed against the chicken coop.

Farley jumped on top of Davy, and the two rolled over and over in the dirt. They crashed into the fence, and the boards smashed beneath them. While Davy sprawled groggily in the splintered wreckage, Wildman grabbed a board and swung it like a club over his head.

But Davy's fist swung faster, and Wildman sank slowly to the ground.

Charley Two Shirts cheered in Cherokee.

Georgie shouted enthusiastically, "An' that goes for me, too!"

Bruno and Henderson exchanged alarmed glances. Henderson quickly cocked his rifle and aimed it at Davy.

A shot rang out.

Suddenly Henderson let out a scream. His rifle clattered to the ground as he grabbed his shoulder in pain. Bruno stared down at his friend in disbelief.

Davy looked around in confusion.

Charley Two Shirts held Davy's still-smoking rifle in his hands. Georgie pointed his rifle at Bruno.

"Hand it over, slowly," Georgie said.

Bruno reluctantly surrendered his rifle and Farley's fancy iron.

Davy prodded Farley with his toe. "Get up!" he said.

Farley just moaned.

"I said, get up!" Davy repeated.

Farley staggered to his feet. Georgie and Charley marched Bruno over to him.

Davy took his rifle back from the Cherokee. "Much obliged, Charley Two Shirts. I reckon if you hadn't fired first, Mrs. Crockett would be wearing black." Then Davy turned to Farley and pointed toward town with his rifle. "All right, let's get started," he ordered.

Bruno was scared. "What do you aim to do with us?"

"Me? Nothing," Davy said through gritted teeth. "But you're going to stand trial. You varmints got a lot to answer for."

CHAPTER 8

Farley refused to answer any questions at his trial, which was held in the one-room schoolhouse, the only building with enough space and chairs. Plenty of townsfolk, however, found the courage to speak the truth. Charley Two Shirts told all about Farley's attack on his family. And even Farley's fancy lawyer, Thaddeus Thorpe, had trouble denying that his client had stolen several horses and cows.

Thorpe was one of the richest men in the territory and the only lawyer for fifty miles around. He strutted in front of the jury of twelve settlers, grinning like a possum in a gray silk suit. He was a well-fed, red-faced man with distinguished silver side whiskers.

But the townsfolk, who had suffered months of Farley's bullying, were not impressed by Thorpe's big words and rich voice. The spectators cheered when the traveling judge announced the jury's verdict: Farley was guilty of assault, theft, and associated lesser crimes, including disturbing the peace. And he wouldn't be a free man for a very long time.

Once the excitement was over, folks left the schoolhouse as happy as kids set loose for summer vacation. Davy was surprised to see a crinkle cross Georgie's brow. "What troubles you?" he asked his friend.

Georgie scratched his head. "What I can't figure," he said, "is why a respected man like Mr. Thorpe would want to defend a low-down snake like Wildman."

Davy shrugged amiably. "Wildman has a right to a fair trial same as anyone else."

"That's correct, Mr. Crockett!" declared Thaddeus Thorpe. He clapped Davy on the back. "You have a fine sense of justice, and I surely do admire you." Thorpe pumped Davy's hand. "Why, a great magistrate like you is wasted in this small territory. I have some powerful friends in Nashville who could find employment worthy of your talents."

Davy frowned.

"Just think of the good a man like you could do in a city like that," Thorpe oozed.

"Davy's doing plenty of good right here," Georgie said. He did not like this city slicker telling Davy what to do and where to live. Besides, he knew Davy didn't want to live all bunched up in a town.

Mr. Thorpe ignored Georgie and smiled at Davy. "Are you fixing to make magistrating a career?"

Davy looked up at the passing clouds. "Right now, I'd like to ease back on the magistrating and get back to cabin building."

"Well, the offer stands," Mr. Thorpe said. "Nashville sure could use a lawman like you."

Davy grinned. "That's mighty nice of you, but Mrs. Crockett could use a cabin, so I'd best be getting back to it."

"Please don't be a stranger," Mr. Thorpe said, pressing a printed visiting card into Davy's hand. "Call on me anytime. That goes for your friend, too."

Mr. Thorpe smiled at Georgie as if noticing him for the first time. Then he bowed and walked away, his expensive silk suit swishing.

"I don't like that feller," Georgie grumbled as Thorpe was a fair distance away.

Davy fingered the fancy visiting card. "Now Georgie, don't go judging a tree by its bark. Mr. Thorpe was just trying to be friendly."

Georgie muttered, "I'd rather be friends with a copperhead snake!"

CHAPTER 9

Charley Two Shirts wanted to thank his new neighbor for saving his home. So the morning after Farley's trial, Charley came riding up the hill on his spotted horse to invite Davy and Georgie for a celebration dinner at his farm.

"Thank you kindly," Davy said. "That's right neighborly of you."

Georgie smiled. "I sure could use a home-cooked meal, now that you mention it."

Charley grinned and rode his horse back down the hill.

Later that day, Davy and Georgie washed up at the stream, then rode over to the Two Shirts farm. As they neared it, the sound of children's laughter drifted toward them on the late afternoon breeze.

When they reached the house, Davy and Georgie saw a group of Cherokee children swatting at a stuffed deerhide ball with sticks. The game looked like so much fun, Davy wished his sons were there to join in.

Short-haired skinny dogs barked and ran after the

children's feet. Davy found himself missing Whirlwind, Bullet, and Blue almost as much as he missed Polly and his children. But he pushed the homesickness from his heart as he patted one of the frisky dogs. Tonight was for celebrating, and something sure smelled good!

Davy followed the savory aromas into the cabin, where iron pots bubbled on the wood stove. Like most frontier cabins, the one-room wooden home was sparsely furnished with little more than a rough plank table, wooden chairs and stools, and wooden pegs on the wall for hanging clothing.

Charley's wife nodded when Davy and Georgie stepped inside. Her face was flushed from standing over the hot stove. She wore a red cotton calico dress, and her long black hair was caught up in a ponytail.

Several Cherokee women were helping her prepare the meal. They, too, were wearing cotton dresses, made from material brought into the territory by white traders. Most of the women wore their hair in long single braids down their backs.

Charley stepped away from a group of men to greet Davy and Georgie. The men wore plain homespun cotton pants as well as colorful turbans and simple one-piece buckskin moccasins.

Georgie smoothed his hair and fingered his dirty buckskin shirt self-consciously. But he quickly forgot his discomfort when Charley introduced Davy and Georgie to the other men. One old man pulled a pipe and tobacco from the pouch on his shoulder belt. He stuffed the bowl of the pipe with Cherokee tobacco, which was mixed with willow bark and sumac leaves to make it mild and smooth.

The old man lit the pipe with a twig from the stove, took a fragrant puff, then passed it to Davy. The bowl was carved to look like a raccoon. Davy grinned at the masked wooden animal face before drawing smoke and handing the pipe to Georgie.

Soon all but one of the men seemed like old friends. Charley's cousin, Virgil, held himself apart from the cheerful group. Georgie noticed that Virgil looked at the floor more than at anyone's face.

At dinnertime Georgie was disappointed to find Charley's unfriendly cousin seated beside him at the long table.

"Might be he's shy," Davy whispered. He nudged Georgie in the ribs. "See if you can get him to small talk with you a mite."

Georgie tried to get Virgil talking, but Virgil kept his eyes on his plate the whole time. Georgie shrugged and turned his attention to the venison stew and savory hominy grits.

A dessert of nuts, berries, and honey-dipped fry bread ended the meal. As Georgie finished his bread, he asked Virgil, "What're you doing in these parts?"

Virgil pretended not to hear him.

"Are you hunting, trapping, looking for a claim to stake,

or just visiting your folks?" Georgie persisted.

Virgil's face grew hard. "Why stake a claim if someone can just cheat you out of it?" he asked angrily.

"Davy saved Charley's claim," Georgie said. "Maybe now that he's magistrate, there won't be any more problems."

But the only reply Virgil gave was a bitter stare. He noisily pushed back his chair, got up, and walked away from the table.

Charley Two Shirts apologized for his cousin's rude behavior. "He has been this way ever since his father lost his land."

Davy sighed. There were bad folks like Farley everywhere, it seemed, making life hard for decent folks. He could see that Charley was embarrassed. The Cherokee people were unfailingly polite to guests.

After many friendly good-byes, Davy and Georgie took their leave. The moon lit their way as they rode across Charley's field to their campsite.

As they rode, they heard bullfrogs croaking on the banks of the creek. Crickets sang their springtime songs. Somewhere a whippoorwill whistled sadly, and a bobwhite chirped its two-note call.

Davy stroked his full stomach and sighed. "Now that's a meal to make a man glad he has teeth." He glanced over at Georgie's wrinkled brow. "What's eating you? Too much hominy?"

Georgie shook his head. "I don't like that Virgil character. Can't help thinking he's up to no good."

Davy picked a piece of corn from his teeth with the tip of his hunting knife. "Maybe so, but I like to give a stranger the benefit of a doubt. Losing your land is enough to make anyone ornery."

CHAPTER 10

Over the next few weeks, Davy's cabin building was slowed down by his official duties as magistrate. Folks trusted Davy because he was honest, and they came to him with all sorts of troubles. Between settling disputes, finding stray cattle, and deciding whose pig was whose, Davy thought he'd never finish that house.

One morning, Davy and Georgie were hard at work stacking notched logs to build the walls of the cabin. They stopped when they heard a horse galloping up the hill.

"Davy Crockett!" shouted Mr. Swaney. The storekeeper's black horse topped the crest of the rise.

"What now?" Georgie groaned. "At this rate we'll never finish building this cabin."

Davy sighed. After the evening at Charley's farm, he'd had a powerful hankering to see Polly and the children.

"Good morning, Mr. Swaney!" Davy called.

"I've seen better," Mr. Swaney said sourly. The store-keeper reined his horse and leaned over. "Hope you don't mind if I keep my seat. With my rheumatism acting up, it took me half the morning getting into the saddle, and I'm due back at the store."

"What brings you up this way?" Georgie asked.

Mr. Swaney shook his head. "Got word from a traveling tinker that there's highwaymen robbing people on the road. Took every one of the poor feller's pots and pans."

"Reckon as magistrate I'll have to catch the varmints," Davy said. It seemed like only yesterday he'd captured Farley and his gang.

Davy laid down his ax and took up his rifle. Thunder rumbled in the distance, and heavy clouds were darkening the sky. He shrugged as he climbed onto his horse. This didn't look like it would have been a good building day anyhow.

"Reckon it's best you don't take on the whole gang alone," said Georgie as he snatched up his rifle. " 'Sides, you ain't leavin' me to finish this whole cabin by myself," he added with a wink.

When Davy and Georgie rode into town, they questioned the unfortunate tinker. He told them he had been traveling along the trail east of the settlement when robbers jumped out at him from the woods on either side of the path.

Georgie shook his head. "Plenty of scrub that way. Those men could be hiding anywhere."

"Then I reckon we best start looking!" Davy said. He swung back up into his saddle.

The two woodsmen easily found the place where the tinker had been robbed. Snapped twigs and scuffed soil showed where the robbers had jumped from cover and attacked.

Davy bent to study the tracks. "Looks like there's about six men, not counting the tinker," he said.

"Six against two." Georgie smiled. "Doesn't seem fair. Maybe you ought to tie one of your hands behind your back."

Davy grinned. "Only if you fight 'em on one foot."

Georgie walked a few steps. "Reckon their trail leads this way?"

Davy nodded. The woods were too thick for the horses, so Davy and Georgie set off on foot. Black crows cawed in the treetops.

Davy and Georgie had spent all their lives tracking critters around in the woods, so they knew what to look for: broken twigs, bent grass, bits of clothing clinging to thorns. The robbers' trail circled round and round, which Davy thought was curious.

"Wouldn't you think they'd just clear off?" Davy muttered.

"Since they're new to these parts, maybe they're lost," Georgie suggested.

Davy frowned. "Or fixin' to rob someone else."

Lightning flashed with a great crack of thunder, and a downpour began to drench the woods.

"That just beats all!" Georgie exclaimed.

Davy smiled. "This'll clean your buckskins."

"And make 'em stick like ice to my skin," Georgie complained. But he tromped on behind Davy.

Davy stopped. "Looks like they've split up here."

And before he could say anything more, the robbers rushed from the bushes, aiming an assortment of pistols and rifles at Davy and Georgie.

"This day just gets better and better," Georgie muttered. He surrendered his rifle to a whiskery robber in a fox hat and blackened cracked buckskins.

Davy caught Georgie's eyes and, with a secret signal, motioned for him to look to his right. Georgie squinted through the drumming rain and recognized Charley Two Shirts's cousin, Virgil, as one of the gang members.

"Let's kill 'em!" cried a tall, skinny man with a long hatchet of a face and eyes so squinty they looked like two short lines. A raggedy top hat perched on his thinning gray hair. He wore an old blue army coat over patched homespun trousers and heavy boots.

"I don't know, Squint," said the robber in the fox cap. "The boss might not..."

"I'm the boss here," Squint growled. "Me. Squint Magee. And don't you forget it, Ferlin!"

Ferlin stepped back and looked nervously at his dirt-caked moccasins.

"I'll kill 'em if you want!" piped up the youngest robber.

He was short and bow-legged, and his tiny blond head was ornamented by two rather large ears. His old buckskin jacket was missing most of its fringe. A rope belt held up his baggy pants, which were rolled up at the bottom, revealing a pair of oversize moccasins. His left big toe waggled out through the top seam. He cocked his rifle eagerly.

"Slow down there, Woody," Squint said. "Ferlin might be right."

"You think you fellers could discuss our fate in a drier spot?" Davy asked.

"Shut up, you!" Squint spit out.

"We could hold them for ransom," Virgil suggested.

"Why, you ungrateful son of a she-cat!" Georgie sputtered.

Virgil ignored him. "The town might pay a pretty price to get its magistrate back. Especially since he's Davy Crockett."

Woody's eyes widened, and his knobby knees almost knocked. "Davy Crockett!"

Squint slowly leaned into Crockett's face. "You ain't so tough," he mumbled. He turned to his men and said, "I reckon we could use the ransom."

Woody scratched his little head. "Don't you think we oughta ask Mr.—"

Squint slapped Woody. "Shut up!"

Davy's brow furrowed. He wondered who they were talking about and hoped he and Georgie would live to find out.

The other two robbers, Hank and Allen, hastened to obey. The robbers used their hunting knives to slice leather thongs from the fringe on their buckskin shirts. They pinned Davy's and Georgie's arms behind their backs and wrapped the thongs tightly around their wrists.

Woody knelt before Davy and started tying a thong around his ankles.

Squint kicked Woody. "What are you doin'? He can't walk to camp like that."

Woody rubbed his sore ribs and blushed.

Squint sighed. "Just shoot 'em if they try to run away. You can do that, can't you?"

"Yes, sir!" Woody said, lifting his heavy rifle.

"Is your gun loaded?" Squint asked sarcastically. Woody looked down at the barrel, and Squint slapped his little head.

"Don't do that! You might blow out what little brains you've got," Squint yelled. "I don't know why I told your momma I'd bring you along."

"I'm sorry, Daddy," Woody whined.

Georgie could hardly keep from laughing. Davy winked at his friend and said quietly under his breath, "We might get to finish that cabin yet!"

CHAPTER 11

The robbers' camp was a messy, muddy circle of crudely made lean-tos. The men had stuck large tree limbs into the ground to make rough frames and had covered them with branches.

The ground was littered with the pots and pans the robbers had stolen from the tinker. Rain pattered musically on the shiny metal. Davy noticed bullet holes in all of them.

"Why steal pots just to shoot 'em?" Davy whispered to Georgie as they were led into camp.

Georgie agreed. "You'd think they'd want to sell them," he quietly replied to Davy.

"Quit your jabberin'!" Squint yelled.

Old greasy chicken bones and half-burned logs filled the growing puddle that had been the robber's campfire. When Squint saw the soggy logs, he threw his hat on the ground in a tantrum.

"Now look at that! The fire's gone out. Fix it up, Virgil!" he yelled.

Davy saw resentment smoldering in the young Cherokee's dark eyes. But Virgil pulled dry wood from beneath an oiled canvas. Davy noticed that Virgil's lean-to was much more carefully built than the rest.

"Make yourselves at home," Squint cackled. He shoved Davy and Georgie, and they fell onto the sopping ground. "*Now* you can tie their feet," Squint told Woody.

"That's right neighborly of you," Davy said as the young man knotted rawhide around his ankles.

"You're awful brave while our hands and feet are tied," Georgie groused.

Squint spit on Georgie, then drew back his narrow head and laughed. "Build the fire," he told his son.

Woody whined. "But Pa! I thought the new man had to build the fire and cook supper."

Squint turned to Virgil and snapped, "Well, what're you waitin' for? Christmas?"

Virgil kept his eyes on the ground as he went silently about his tasks. Davy looked at Georgie. They were both wondering why he had joined the gang.

Ferlin took a sickly-looking rabbit and a couple of squirrels from his game pouch and gave them to Virgil to cook. Virgil was soon spooning stew into battered tin bowls. Squint stopped him from serving food to the prisoners.

"Ain't enough to go 'round," Squint said. " 'Sides, nohow are we going to untie 'em. And I ain't about to spoon-feed 'em like babies."

Georgie whispered to Davy, "Don't mind missing that scrawny mess."

Ferlin patted his rifle proudly. "You're not the only hunter around here," he sneered at Davy.

"If you was really that good with a rifle, you'd be bringing in one of those fat bears," Georgie said with contempt.

Ferlin wiped the grease from his mouth. "I reckon rabbit's better'n nothing, and nothing's what you got!" he snorted.

"We'll be eating steak once they pay your ransom," Squint cackled. Rain dripped off his hat brim and ran down his narrow face. "Could you go fetch the jug, Virgil," Squint said.

Virgil went silently to Squint's lean-to. He came back carrying a chipped clay jug.

Squint pulled out the corncob stopper and took a long swallow. He coughed and choked and smacked his lips with satisfaction, then passed the jug to Hank. When Woody reached for it, Squint slapped his hand.

"What would your ma say?"

Davy watched the jug's progress around the circle. Escape would be easier with drunken guards. But he noted with disappointment that Virgil did not drink.

The fire sputtered miserably in the rain, which had dwindled to a nasty, cold drizzle.

Allen wiped his filthy, wet face with his equally wet and dirty sleeve. "Miserable wet weather," he grumbled.

"You think this rain is bad?" Georgie scoffed. "Once, me and Davy were caught in a rain so wet it washed half of Tennessee into Alabama."

"Really?" Woody asked. His lower lip hung open.

"Shut your jaw before you catch flies," Squint snapped.

Davy nodded. "Rain was so heavy, we couldn't find the path beneath our feet. Then we couldn't find the woods. Then we couldn't find ourselves! Might've drowned if we hadn't been lucky enough to meet up with a passel o' alligators."

Ferlin looked skeptically at Davy. "The gators didn't eat you?"

Georgie shook his head. "Davy was too fast for 'em."

Davy grinned. "It was Georgie's singin' that threw the critters off. They was so busy listening, I had time to tie 'em all together with my rope and make a tolerable good raft. Till a house floated by and we figured that'd be more comfortable."

Squint frowned at Woody. "Don't fill your head with such nonsense."

"T'ain't nonsense," Georgie said. " 'Sides, don't you want to know what happened when the house hit the rapids?"

Woody's blue eyes widened.

"Time for sleep!" Squint yelled.

Woody whispered to Davy. "Promise to tell me about the rapids tomorrow, Mr. Crockett?"

Davy hesitated just long enough to build up suspense, as he liked to do with his sons back home. Then he grinned. "Sure as sunrise," he said.

"Ferlin, you take the first watch," Squint commanded. He rolled up in a mangy blanket and fell to snoring almost immediately. The other robbers settled into their lean-tos.

Ferlin sat with his back to the crackling campfire so he wouldn't be blinded by its light. He hummed to himself to keep awake.

Georgie whispered, "That young feller gave me an idea. Keep 'em interested in your yarn, Davy, and they might not be so ready to turn out our lights."

A slow smile spread across Davy's face. "Folks sure do love stories," he agreed. "Couldn't hurt to try."

CHAPTER 12

Dawn came, but with no sign of the sun. The dull sky
just grew lighter. Low clouds carried the threat of
more rain.

After a soggy breakfast, Squint swirled the dregs of coffee in his cup.

"Get moving, Ferlin. You go into town and tell them hillbillies if they want to see Crockett alive, they're gonna have to pay."

"Sure thing," Ferlin said.

Davy and Georgie watched Ferlin vanish into the dripping woods. They could hear him splashing for quite a while.

"Now all we have to do is wait," Squint said, taking a pull off his jug. "You two better hope them clodhoppers cough up some money, or you'll wind up like that other magistrate."

"How's that?" Davy asked innocently. He wondered how these men knew about the man he replaced.

"Let's just say you'll find out, if Ferlin don't come back with some cash money," Squint cackled.

Hours passed, but there was no sign of Ferlin. Water dripped from the canopy of leaves. The occasional blue jay screeched, but most of the forest silently waited for a better day.

Georgie wriggled uncomfortably in his cold buckskins. He felt hungry enough to eat a log. His stomach growled like a pack of wolves.

"Looks like Ferlin's not coming back," Davy said. "Reckon you underestimated them good folks. For all you know they're getting a posse together this very minute. I calculate it's best if you let us go right now."

Squint sneered. "I calculate you best mind your own business, or soon you'll be one dead magistrate."

Georgie said, "You don't seem to be too good at business. How do you figure on making a profit off them pots and pans if you shoot 'em full of holes?"

"Don't need to sell 'em," Squint replied.

"Then how do you figure this robbery business is gonna pay off?" Georgie asked.

"I got ways," Squint snickered. "I've got bigger fish to fry than a few iron skillets."

Davy wished he could scratch his head, but his hands were still tied firmly behind his back. He wiggled his fingers, trying to chase the numbness from his hands.

"Then why steal 'em in the first place?" Davy wondered.

Squint spit and stood up. "Maybe tradesmen ain't wanted in these parts. If there ain't no tradesmen, then there's nothing for folks to trade their crops for. If the crops are worthless, what good is their land? Reckon they'd have to pick up and move on."

Davy studied Squint's narrow face. "I calculate you mean someone might pay some good old boys like you and Wildman to run folks out of the territory. And that someone could take over all those claims. A body could get mighty rich that way."

Squint chuckled. "You're a smart man, Mr. Crockett. But all your smarts ain't gonna help you none. A man who knows a lot can't talk about any of it when he's dead. Why, I might just take that ransom and put a bullet in you anyway."

"But he ain't finished his story, Pa," Woody objected.

Squint looked disgusted and picked up his rifle. "Hank, Allen. Let's go find some game," he muttered.

The two rangy robbers got to their feet.

"Virgil, you and Woody watch these two. And whatever you do, don't untie 'em," Squint warned. The hunting party headed into the damp woods.

"Can I hear about the rapids now?" Woody asked eagerly.

Virgil frowned. "You go get more wood for the fire."

"But Pa said...," Woody protested.

Virgil's black eyes stared at the young man. Woody swallowed hard. "Yes, sir, Mr. Virgil, sir."

The young man loped into the woods.

Virgil sat down beside Georgie and Davy. He was about to speak when Woody popped out of a bush. "Forgot my ax," Woody explained.

Georgie sighed. "Some folks would forget their heads if they weren't tied on."

The faintest smile creased the corners of Virgil's lips. Davy looked deeply into the Cherokee's dark eyes.

"What is a man like you doing with these scalawags?" Davy asked after Woody disappeared into the brush.

Virgil scanned the woods before he answered. Rifles boomed in the distance. "These are the men who ran my father off his land. I have joined their gang to bring them to justice."

Georgie whistled. "No wonder you didn' t want to tell me what you were doing in these parts."

"Well, how do you reckon on doing that?" Davy wondered. "There's just one of you and five of them."

"This scheme is bigger than these men," Virgil said. "You could hang them all, and the land stealing would still go on."

"Well, I figured there was a connection between them and Farley," Davy said. "Varmints like them usually just move along, robbing as they go. But these gangs are staying put in this territory—and they're more set on driving good folks away than they are on stealing. I calculate they must be working for someone who's making it worth their while to stick around."

Virgil nodded in agreement. "But I have not yet learned who their boss is. The men still do not trust me."

Davy stroked his chin thoughtfully. "There might be a way to loosen their tongues. After a dog gets a raccoon up a tree, he starts barkin'. If we let these boys think we're licked, they just might talk. Old Squint's already begun a bit of howlin'."

Virgil looked puzzled. Georgie shrugged. "Don't look at me. Davy's the one with the plan."

More rifle fire boomed somewhere in the hills.

"All right, now listen up here," Davy said. The three men leaned their heads together and whispered.

Suddenly Virgil held up a hand for silence. Someone was approaching through the brush.

Woody stumbled into camp, struggling under an armload of logs. He tripped over a root, and the logs scattered all over.

Virgil picked them up and brought them near the fire to dry. Woody smiled gratefully.

It was early evening by the time Squint, Hank, and Allen came back with a groundhog and more squirrels. The hunters carefully stashed their long rifles under an oilskin in one of the lean-tos to keep them from the rain.

"Bet you'd like to have some of this," Squint taunted, waving a pair of dead squirrels in Davy's face.

"Reckon I'm hungry enough to eat my own moccasins," Davy said.

"Well, you can't have none till you beg," Squint jeered.

"Reckon I'm not that hungry," Davy declared. "Humble pie's too hard too digest."

"Where's your friend Ferlin?" Georgie asked.

Squint kicked, but Georgie swerved away from the thick

boot. "Virgil, cook these up," Squint ordered, tossing the squirrels to the Cherokee.

Soon the robbers were scraping the last of Virgil's stew from their tin bowls. Georgie thought there was no greater torment than smelling hot stew and not being able to taste even a bite of it. He could hear Davy's stomach growling like an old bear, but Davy never let on that he was the least bit uncomfortable.

Woody wiped the stew from his thin lips. "What about the rapids, Mr. Crockett? You promised, remember?"

Davy smiled. "Well, it was nothin' really. The river started rising and tossing, roiling and a-boiling, till we thought that old house we were floating on would come apart at the foundation. So I grabbed a ceiling beam and tied a big sheet to it for a sail, and I made the back door into a rudder for old Georgie. Then we whistled up a wind...."

Davy winked at Georgie, and the two of them whistled. Some of the robbers laughed, but Squint scowled and mumbled.

Davy continued. "We were having a grand time sailing those rapids till I looked up and saw a comet heading straight for the sails. Well, that was no good, 'cause it'd burn up the sails, and we'd already used all the sheets in the house. So I reached up and grabbed that comet and wrung the tail right off it."

Woody gasped.

Davy grinned. "It singed the hair off my hat and burned my hands a mite. But when the smoke cleared, we were safe. I figured that the flood would never go down, so I started to drink that river dry. I was about halfway done when a boat full of pirates came rowing toward us. Those varmints demanded all we had, down to the door latch. But Georgie and I refused. We'd taken a shine to that house and were fixing to live in it once things dried out. So we stood our ground. And the pirate captain said, 'Shoot 'em, boys!' And they let fly with powder and ball! It was a regular lead blizzard. Why, them bullets were whizzing around us like bees at a honey tree."

"What happened then?" Woody asked in open-mouthed wonder.

Davy yawned. "Well, I reckon that'll have to wait till tomorrow."

The robbers groaned with disappointment. And even though Woody begged and said, "Pretty please with molasses on top," Davy just closed his eyes and soon began to snore.

Virgil volunteered to stand guard for the night. The robbers found their blankets and quickly began snoring, too. After they were all asleep, the Cherokee crept around the camp to complete his part of the escape plan.

Virgil silently slipped them some beef jerky, parched corn, and water.

"Tastes mighty fine," Georgie whispered.

"Can't compare to Polly's cooking, but it sure is welcome," Davy agreed.

CHAPTER 13

The next morning, the clouds parted and a red sunrise gleamed on the dew. Bird songs greeted the new day. Davy and Georgie pretended that their arms and legs were still tied together. Woody was up with the sun, pestering Davy to finish the story. "How come the pirates didn't kill you if they was that close and firing all those bullets?" Woody asked.

Davy yawned and blinked. "Why, we caught the bullets, of course."

Woody's jaw dropped to his chest. The other bandits laughed and slapped their knees.

Hank wiped tears of laughter from his eyes. Crockett sure was a funny man. It was going to be a shame to kill him!

Woody eased closer to Davy and Georgie.

"You can catch bullets, can't you?" Georgie asked.

Woody scratched his tiny head.

"Boy, they're making a fool of you, and it's an easy job," Squint grumbled.

"Well, catching bullets does take a lot of practice, and I wouldn't recommend trying it at night," Davy allowed. "But me and Georgie, we're bullet catchers from way back."

"Well, you're gonna catch some of mine right now," Squint snarled. "Seein' as how Ferlin ain't come back, I figure you ain't worth keepin' alive no more, anyhow."

"Now why would a smart man like you be willing to swing from a gallows just to do someone else's work?" Davy asked.

Squint blinked his narrow eyes. "How do you figure that?" he demanded crossly.

"Well, hanging's the punishment for murder, and you ain't even got a grudge against me," Davy drawled. "So I figure you're taking orders from someone else. You ain't the boss, after all!"

"Me and Thorpe are partners fifty-fifty!" Squint yelled.

"Pa!" Woody gasped. "You said we couldn't tell."

Squint growled. "It don't matter now," he said. "Dead men tell no tales." He reached for his rifle.

"It's a fine day for bullet catchin'!" Davy hollered. He and Georgie leapt to their feet and stretched out their arms. The leather thongs dropped to the ground. For an instant Squint froze in his tracks. Then he aimed his rifle straight at Davy's chest.

"Shoot 'em, boys!" he screeched. And his rifle thundered. The other men were too surprised to move.

Davy reached in the air like he was grabbing something.

Then he tossed a bullet right back at Squint. The lead pellet knocked the robber's hat off his head.

Squint blinked in amazement.

"Told you I could catch 'em," Davy said.

While the robbers were motionless with shock, Virgil quickly pulled Davy and Georgie's rifles from the bushes and tossed them to his friends. They leveled rifles at Squint and his gang.

"Now, let's see how good you are at catching bullets," Davy said. " 'Course, if you'd rather come along peaceable, that's all the same to me."

"How did you do that?" Squint marveled.

Davy grinned and showed the villain a palm full of bullets. "Why, Virgil here emptied your guns last night. You were shooting nothing but powder."

"Virgil!" Squint shrieked.

"You should have known better than to steal his father's land," Georgie said.

Davy, Georgie, and Virgil marched the band of robbers to the main trail, where they rounded up Soapy and Lightning. Then Squint and his gang were led back to town, Thaddeus Thorpe was arrested, and a messenger was sent to bring the traveling judge.

A few days later, Davy was cutting the door in his finished cabin when Mr. Swaney rode up the hill to tell him he was needed in town for the trial. "This should really be something, Davy," Mr. Swaney said. "Ol' Thaddeus Thorpe was madder'n a wet hen when he was arrested."

Davy grinned. "I reckon he's not used to being on the receiving end of a trial."

"Wait'll he hears what Squint and the others have to say," Georgie added. "They'll be glad to send Thorpe to jail if it means less time for them."

Davy nodded. "Reckon Farley'll be coming back for a whole new trial—this time for killing that other magistrate. Seems a shame that poor man had to die just because Mr. Thorpe got greedy. Some folks just can't see past their own pockets."

Mr. Swaney nodded. "That's why we need the law. Speaking of which, we'll be needing someone to run for colonel of the militia. Mr. Thorpe had his eye on the job, but now he's tied up."

Georgie chuckled.

"What about you, Davy?" Mr. Swaney asked.

"Colonel Crockett." Davy laughed. "I kinda like the sound of it."

Georgie grinned. "While you're dreaming, how about Congressman Crockett?"

Davy glanced at the nearly finished cabin. "I reckon I oughta finish our cabin first!"

EPILOG

Davy Crockett is perhaps the most famous folk hero of the American frontier. He was born in 1786 and grew up in the rugged country of eastern Tennessee, where his father ran a small country inn. Business was never very good, and the family often relied on young Davy's hunting skills to put food on the table. But even in rough times, Davy had a knack for amusing himself and others with tall tales, a skill that was to later become part of the Crockett legend.

In 1806, Davy married Polly Finley, and they began to raise a family. As the frontier grew more crowded with settlers, Davy and Polly kept moving their family farther west. In 1813, Davy and his family moved for the last time, deep into western Tennessee.

Davy championed the rights of Native Americans in an era marked by great injustice toward Indian people. In 1813, he joined the army in an effort to negotiate an end to the Creek War. His efforts were successful, and in the process he earned the respect of both sides.

Davy returned from the war a hero and was so popular that he was eventually elected to the United States Congress, where he served three terms. During that time, he helped draft a treaty that would have enabled the Indian people to keep their land. But in 1835, when Congress decided to break the treaty and his efforts to save it failed, he decided not to run for reelection.

In 1836, Davy Crockett, along with his trusted companion Georgie Russel, joined a small band of brave American settlers under siege at the Alamo in San Antonio, Texas, which was then part of Mexico. The settlers fought long and valiantly in the name of freedom to defend themselves against the Mexican army, but in the end their numbers were no match for the huge force amassed against them. The enemy soldiers finally overran the Alamo, killing many men, women, and children within its walls. Davy Crockett died as he had lived—as an American hero. And the phrase "Remember the Alamo!" lived on to inspire and unite the Americans in Texas, who eventually won their freedom from Mexico and brought Texas into the United States.